POETICS OF WORK

POETICS OF WORK

Noémi Lefebvre

Translated from the French by
Sophie Lewis

**TRANSIT
BOOKS**

Published by Transit Books
2301 Telegraph Avenue, Oakland, California 94612
www.transitbooks.org

Originally published in French as *Poétique de l'emploi*
by Éditions Verticales © Éditions gallimard, Paris, 2018
Translation copyright © Sophie Lewis, 2020

First published in English translation by Transit Books in 2021.

Every effort has been made to trace and acknowledge copyright for materials
appearing in the book.

ISBN: 978-1-945492-44-0 (paperback)
LIBRARY OF CONGRESS CONTROL NUMBER: 2020951933

DESIGN & TYPESETTING
Justin Carder

DISTRIBUTED BY
Consortium Book Sales & Distribution
(800) 283-3572 | cbsd.com

Printed in the United States of America

9 8 7 6 5 4 3 2

This work received support from the French Ministry of Foreign Affairs and
the Cultural Services of the French Embassy in the United States through their
publishing assistance program.

 This project is supported in part by a grant from the National
Endowment for the Arts.

POETICS OF WORK

1

The wind was in the north and the planes were circling, the shops were open for the love of everything under the sun, riot police were patrolling four by four and junior officers by threes out in the streets.

There isn't a lot of poetry these days, I said to my father.

I said that like a feeling or perhaps an opinion, not like an idea, not categorically anyway, it was so my father could appreciate the funny side of this new climate within me, and I should admit I was under the influence of books and in the sway of drugs, I'd smoked while reading Klemperer and read Kraus while eating bananas and reread Klemperer while smoking a fair bit more, his diary from start to finish and especially *The Language of the Third Reich: LTI*. With the Klemperer I spent hours fixated on just one moment out of the whole Third Reich, from the start in fact, summed up by a line that I read and reread in order to grasp its magnitude: *Some kind of fog has descended which is enveloping everybody.*

My father was in his four-wheel drive, seated nobly above the everyday, he was adjusting the rearview to suit his sightline while at the same time conducting a concerto in C-sharp minor, he was also coding the results of sequencing the genome and debating the foundations of value, he was digging the land with peasants in the Ardèche, he was writing his essay on scholastic philosophy, visiting children with cancer, saving people from drowning in the Mediterranean, watching TV in his boxers, giving his universal blood, trimming his nails while reading Sophocles, he was handsome and dignified. At last he said

"How do you know if there's poetry around or not, plenty of poetry or not much? You want to measure the quantity of poetry but do you even know what poetry is?"
"Maybe not, Papa."

"And even if poetry experts were able to measure a standard concentration of poetry and confirm a trend of rarefication, how could you establish that this rarefying trend in poetry levels has any connection with what's going on at the moment?"
"I couldn't, Papa."

"Don't you think it's rather bad taste to talk about poetry at this particular juncture?"
"Yes, Papa."

"Aren't there more urgent problems?"
"There are, Papa."

"Having killed nearly 300,000 broadly ferocious beasts, among them thousands of seagulls and a few hundred kangaroos, Archduke Franz Ferdinand dragged us all into a world war by getting himself shot like a rabbit. And you're fussing over poetry."
"I'm not fussing, Papa."

"What earthly good is poetry when lunatics filled with global hatred are blowing their brains out amid crowds of ordinary people?"
"Indeed, Papa."

"With distant wars lapping at our doorsteps? With Europe assailed by doubt and Greek debt?"
"All the more, Papa."

"Shouldn't we first and foremost secure the Freedom that is prerequisite for the exercise of our basic rights, among which, for example, the right to compose poetry when the whim takes us?"

"But who is this we, Papa? Who are you talking about—the people who live around here? Fervent patriots? Average citizens?"

"Work it out for yourself!"

If by that he meant that everything had turned serious and consequently that no one could be bothered to care about poetry, I was pretty much in agreement seeing as poets annoy me generally, so I'd have preferred not to discuss it, but my father was just beginning to enjoy himself with his insincere stand on national unity while also leafing through the good city of Lyon's own newspaper *Le Progrès*.

"At a time when the police and the army are watching over our Liberty, how can you claim we're short of poetry? Isn't that evidence of a low-down and frankly defeatist state of mind?"

I'd made the mistake of imagining poetry as the freedom to say whatever you like, independent of any attacks on the Republic or shadows looming over Democracy, my father explained in the groove of his lecturing style, I was defending this completely groundless view quite unmoored from the reality of our changing times while it was in fact Liberty, yes, that same Liberty to be found on the pediments of school gates and the façades of all the ancient institutions around here which were once threatened by Civilization's enemies, that is by the enemies of the West and therefore of Europe, even of the Republic but first of France herself, which meant . . .

"What did it mean, Papa?"

Him: It meant that the poets had new duties, that they too had to contribute, from now on they would write in the hallowed national realm of liberal Europe's defence; it meant that poetry was summoned freely to defend the freedom of the market economy and primarily of France in the global race of the globalized globe, so if I preferred to hang on to my vague and completely unfounded sense of a poetry deficit, if I preferred to fixate on a romantic and outmoded notion of this useless and entirely futureless non-profession, it was because I myself was, as I should one of these days admit, a shiftless loser too, wasn't I? Can't you simply tell your father that you're anxious about finding a job?

"Ok, fair enough."

"Can't you admit that the more you fret about finding a job, the more you then fret about having a job should you ever actually get one, even while fretting about not finding one?"

I was watching people crossing the Place Bellecour, the statue of Louis XIV loomed over the space, history weighs heavily. We don't have enough nature.

"There's lime blossom in the air, Papa. Can you smell it?"
"Tell your poet friends about it, not me, that'll interest them."

"I don't have friends, Papa, no poets nor anyone else."
"There you go again: moan, moan, moan."

And my father dug his heels into the flanks of his all-terrain pure-breed, the price of which exceeds middle-class comprehension, and in less than thirty seconds he had vanished at a gallop. The time it took me to roll a one-rizla joint. I've been cutting down, recently. I've found a way of drawing out the effects without putting more in, you have to focus on letting your focus go and imagine your ideas in a field of beetroot. Crows were marching to nobody's orders, clouds were racing their threadbare shadows over the woods and plains, still uncharted topographies were fading away under satellite eyes, and the dense air muffled the thousands of voices borne noiselessly along the infinite extensions of wifi, opinions and the mob, the mob and the crowd, the crowd and the masses, the masses and the classes, what's the use thinking about it if your father's hightailing out, as in the times of the three estates, bareback-riding the old banger in your lumpish brain? The category of socio-professional feels unreal, resistance is an electrical idea, the vocabulary is going blind, the subject is under surveillance, there's nothing doing with the verb, the possessive is in the hands of those who can afford it, oh I'd love to eat something that would bung my flow, bananas or spuds or a plateful of pasta and drink milk through a straw or give a cow a big hug, a little one on my level with dewy eyes, the whole scene in a camembert-box meadow, I'll stroll on circular and pasteurised paths beside a limpid river and drooping willows, the very last place to go wondering if there's poetry around or not at the moment.

"Come on, I was teasing."
"I realized, Papa."

Bikes, old people, kids, technology, springtime—none this can generate even the feeling of a future.

"Actually whether you're talking about poetry or something else, I have to say that it doesn't matter at all."

"Of course not, Papa."

"Since you don't matter at all."
"I know."

"Your life doesn't matter, the Universe doesn't matter, the purveyors of legitimate violence are what matter above all and the consequences of these irresponsible characters' importance are so considerable that all you can say to it is really nothing at all."
"Thanks, Papa, I already know all that, you've told me a hundred times and every time it makes me want to do myself in."

My father highlighted my state of depression, he theorised about the banality of the malaise spreading first among those who have all they need to be happy while others have nothing and are happy anyway, but as psychological questions have never been his forte, he went to order sushi and drink saké and sing "Let it be" in a karaoke club with great-value sweet and giggly girls or I don't know who else accustomed to being paid for their excellent company, no matter, when he got back he was in better spirits.

"Now I'm all ears."

I didn't know what to say. Honestly I had nothing to say, I must have been looking for a reason to fret, as I always do, or to brood, as I ought to admit, because everything's okay out there in the shops, people are looking normal, there is this fashion for wearing combat prints and the army working hard at marching ever so softly when they're only kids of twenty but, for all that, it still doesn't feel much like the DRC or Syria or Pakistan or South Sudan, while still not quite being Switzerland either.

"Are we at war, Papa?"
"What makes you think that?"
"I don't know, all these soldiers outside the shops."
"Then it must be war."

"But people are shopping in the sales."
"So we can't be at war."

"The police are checking handbags and ID cards."
"That means it's war."

"But there are no tanks or any shelling on our good city of Lyon."
"It's not war, then."

"There are troops on the ground."

"Then it is war."

"But there's no fighting."
"That's because we're not at war."

"People are afraid, Papa."
"Because we're at war."

"I wonder if the flameproof feline regulation camo-wear in the city center of our good city of Lyon is not a strategic mistake. If the idea is to melt into the urban scene, anyway, that's bombed."
"That's because we're not at war."

"I guess the army has to be visible for the sake of se-curity?"
"Because we're at war."

"Hence the combat camouflage on the catwalk for next season's fashions?"
"Because nonetheless we're not at war."

"But there are posters everywhere about the army's recruitment drive, and the army's here for war, right?"

"You should buy yourself a chicken sandwich. And pick up a strawberry smoothie for me."

People were handing out flyers on the rue Victor-Hugo, it's a shopping street, never without a few prophets to announce the good news of rock-bottom prices and miracle products, it's an earthly mission that brings almost no reward, the key is to believe in it, these prophets wear the smiles of the market economy otherwise they'll be sacked; this is the slavery of voluntary labour, or so it seems, that's why I always say hello nicely, no thanks without malice and goodbye without complaint. That said, I noticed, my father too, that the smile of a girl approaching me was much too radiant for the face of employment. There was no clear sign but something considered in her way of collaring passersby suggested the energy of hidden depths.

"They're fascists," my father said.

"You're fascists!" I said to the girl, with all due respect to my father.

"No we're not fascists," the girl replied unfazed, as if expecting this remark, which would be quite insulting for anyone not a fascist; she didn't seem to find it very terrible and indeed it wasn't exactly a hanging crime. It was simple and very sensible, popular and basic, what she was giving the innocent locals to read: *this is our home*, that's all.

"She's a cultural spokesperson for the local fascist hierarchy; they're the worst, you have to give them hell." My father turned again and shouted: "Fascists!"

"Fascists!" I echoed, more softly, once they were too far to hear.

As I had nothing more urgent to think about, I wondered what they meant by *our home*. Perhaps *our home* was this crossroads where we were, between the pharmacy, the Crédit Agricole bank, the Arab corner store and the clothes shop, or perhaps it was the whole pedestrianized street.

"Not a doubt," my father said.
"Further than the street? The neighborhood, then; the city, France, Europe . . ."
"Doubtless . . ."
"And following on logically, then Planet Earth too . . ."
"No doubt, no doubt . . ."

My father says no doubt when he has doubts, it's a way of making me doubtful through expression of the good and sober concern that sometimes arises, in a new circumstance, from the lucidity of those rare minds we call critics. As I often return to my own case, I was wondering whether *this is our home* included me too, wondering if the girl meant she was at home in my home, and who wasn't at home, in our home, with her, at mine, if it was the people of this Planet Earth or extraterrestrials. I was wondering if being at home meant calling those who aren't at home extraterrestrials, Martians for example, though they don't exist. My father raised a finger and quoted Zhuangzi, then standing in the middle of the Place Ampère, precleared of mendicancy thanks to the denunciatory zeal of the residents of this historic district for Catholicism and the Vichy Milice, he declared that if the question was *who was at our home in our home* there was an answer to that: it was *we* who were. And he added that if the question was *where was home* that too had its answer: it was *wherever we were*. Fair enough, I conceded, but we didn't know who *we* were nor why it was *at home* where *we* were. What did they understand by that?

"They understand that you'll understand their understandings. They intend you to double-intend all their filthy double-entendres with them."

I walked on in silence.
My father had his four-wheel drive on a long lead, it's pleasant when he's stepped out and is ambling slowly beside his beast.

"There's something that frightens me, Papa."
"What?"
"That girl, actually, I was thinking, she's the outcome of an education . . ."

"I don't know what you're going on about."

"If I may, without meaning to judge anyone, in a strictly general way and with no connection to you or me or this business between us about which I've absolutely no intention of talking . . ."

"Go ahead, speak, please."
"You won't blow up at me?"
"Of course not."
"Education starts with the family—that's what I'm thinking."

"Then we need to know what that family is made of. What is its class, and its community? Who talks about community anyway?"

I had nothing to say to that.
"Who ever made a serious survey of this notion of a community?"
"I have no idea, Papa."

"No one. Besides me. And, in full possession of the facts, this is how I see it: we have two communities, one of dubious social standing at best, and another one as shady as the first."

"But there's the heart of the community, I wouldn't say this holds true everywhere and at all times, but in particular social circles perpetuated by an education, and this social circle is still and always traditionally founded upon . . ."

At this my father began to spin like a dervish, delivering corner kicks to both sides of my brain, to my temples, sinuses and even the backs of my eyes, my battered brain cried out Okay Papa okay not the family not the family! We don't care a bit for the family! I was yelling the whole truth about the family which means nothing and produces nothing that's meaningful, ever, which is completely irrelevant to political, moral, social and psychological problems, just so he'd stop hitting me but he went on beating me blue to the point of migraine and, as that still wasn't enough, he singled out my rudeness, he cited an article of the penal code in reference to my chronic hopelessness and the relevant penalties for recidivism. I'm used to it, I know I'm a lifer.

2

For years everything that's gone through my head has been debated in this courtroom that I call the house of the dead, where my father presides. Some people talk to God, others to their dogs; my father is my dog, my god, the magistrate who nips at my arse and straightens out my soul, who protects me from all kinds of wanderings and who keeps me from doing life. The call to order is within his remit but he's also the king of jurisprudence, the inventor of obligations I must fulfil and prohibitions I must respect in order to become what he wishes but I don't know what he wishes. How could I know, I never see him.

For a long time I wanted to be rid of him since he wasn't around, but my father shines brightest by his absence. Last year I still wanted to live like other people without my father and leave my father behind by being with other people, I spent evenings in the

company of people who had no connection, neither
close nor remote, with this upholding of the symbol-
ic function that historically identifies authority with
the figurehead of its institution and vice versa, people then with no obligation to answer to him or be
worthy of him but who could let themselves go and
say anything at all, *idiotic things for example*, my father
remarked, could spin *endless observations about issues
of zero interest*, he preferred not to comment, while
reserving his opinion, *producing and reproducing a kind
of tirade as naïve as it is boring*, which transformed, as
the hours filled with marijuana smoke, into *a more or
less continuous flow of sub-philosophical argumentation of
a rare vacuousness,* when it wasn't simply *counter-truths
produced by the zeitgeist*, he would listen to himself talk
while also reading *Marie-Claire* at the dentist, L'Oréal,
Givenchy, Exclusive: Blondes Take the Front Line,
Fashion Week: Armani, Chanel, Sun Capital, Fashion: Balenciaga Dresses the Police, Eros of the Heroes, Society: The Poor are Poor and Rape Hurts,
Pineapple Miracle Fruit, Skincare, Books: The Priz-
es, Psychology: Changing your Habits, Stars: Today
Mercury enters the unconventional sign of Aquari-
us and from this point on you will find yourself well
equipped to surprise others with unpredictable moods
or strange ideas, no change on the emotional side but
that shouldn't, in any case, affect the direction things

are taking, Cancer on the lookout for all opportunities to broaden your professional horizons with savvy! While my father was cultivating himself solo, I was holding conversations without a hint of decency or sense and unfortunately my heart wasn't really in it, in fact I was repeating yes yesses and yeahs and now and then adding a judicious notwithstanding, I was using the present to talk about the past and the conditional for the future not keeping my tenses in agreement at all, he must have noticed my lowered lids and open mouth, lulled by the music of the three-speed dental de-scaler of a great defender of hidden charges and of some people's right to eternally white teeth. Pleased with his enamel and with this opportunity to point out the constant disappointment which, it therefore seemed to him, however chockful his diary, without fail, I felt the need to expose him to, he had prescribed me nearly a hundred years of solitude.

Thanks to my father, I suffer from a physical inadequacy in all things social. Whoever contemplates me sees my father settled in my apartment as if in his own; he's there in my eyes, he hunches my shoulders, slows my stride, spreads out before me his superior grasp of all living things. I'm used to it but people aren't into it, that's natural for people. I understand them, people; my father doesn't understand that I understand people, he's careful to keep reminding me of the difference between me and other people so I won't become someone among people but always nobody among nobody. When I venture a joke or let's say a witticism, my father ensures that the general ridicule silences me on the spot. When I'm asked an ordinary question, I go down rabbit holes of general formulae and elucidations entirely shaped in my father's words, people listen to my father with stricken faces, then comes the dismayed silence. Sometimes I follow up with a little backtracking line, hoping to show that this isn't me, that I'm much funnier and actually rather free-thinking at heart, and people stare at me with sympathy and change the subject, and my father guffaws so loudly that I withdraw my claim to a part in the conversation which is in any case an art and an education, anyway if I was a recognised couch case on docto-psy.com we could call this a rift between the desire to be an entirely independent social being and the inability to do so without my father. While I bring my superego back home, *my soul filled with shame and anger,* as my father says winding me up, I still have to hear him totting up my pathetic parties and reiterating how my friends, as I like to call them, are not friends given that I, according to him and by all accounts, am incapable of friendship, and to listen to him further explicate friendship, its definition and applications, citing the unexcelled example of Montaigne and La Boétie, and those remarkable friendships between Bouvard and Pécuchet, Laurel and Hardy, and Mole and Rat, between Marx and Engels, Calvin and Hobbes, and Mercier and Camier, not forgetting Tintin and Captain Haddock, friends go in pairs, sometimes in threes or fours à la Musketeers, and after that there's Facebook, is that what you want, then, Facebook friends? I'm not listening to him now, I'm out of there into the shitty gales and this fucked-up autumn.

Lesson one: *Poets, subject no one to the authority of a father.*

Paternal authority is, of all authorities, the one most inimical to poetry.

"Are you giving lessons to poets?"
"No—yes . . ."
"In what capacity?"
"None, Papa."

"Did someone ask your advice?"
"No one."

"Do you even know any poets? Are you acquainted with a single true poet?"

"Dunno, maybe not."

"And if, by an extraordinary piece of luck—which is of course no more than a nursery-school hypothesis—there proved to be a poet, a genuine and excellent poet, with whom you speak, why should he, this excellent poet, have any use for your advice?"
"Yes, that was stupid, Papa."

My father is right because he's objective and he's objective because he isn't prey to the fondness that clouds the judgement of most fathers; everything he says to me is impartial.

Impartiality is a Protestant quality in my father, distantly inherited from a tragic ancestor in the Hundred Years War, a comrade-in-arms to the King of Navarre and future King of France, Henri IV, all hobbyhorses pertaining to the aforementioned royal to boot. This quality of my father therefore predates the publication of the great Emmanuel Kant's *Critique of Judgement* which merely disseminated my father's impartiality to the masses, as my father's biographers should be aware, for *this philosopher whom we tend just to call Kant*, whom my father calls *Emmanuel* and not *Immanuel* for all affectation is against his principles, the famous Emmanuel, then, has merely passed on the impartiality of the tragic ancestor from the Hundred

Years War whose nose my father has also inherited and perhaps too his taste for longwinded storytelling. *Kant invented nothing*, that's what you should know, because, however tragic, my father's ancestor was already sitting pretty. Nonetheless *Emmanuel, the happy Protestant*, so my father calls him ironically or in counterpoint to the tragic author of the authors of his days, impossible to say which, *Emmanuel the famous, whom we just call Kant, was certainly a dedicated pen-pusher*, my father admitted, for in all his writings the happy Protestant was pushing impartiality, even though this loftily conceived virtue has not yet, alas, gained the understanding of telephone salespeople. Notwithstanding *Kant full stop*, my father conceded*, did even so write the instruction manual to an aesthetic that we must admit is indispensable to understanding the art of detachment through contemplation*. We can call that indifference.

Indifference is a contemplative state, my father said one day when he'd been drinking.

Contemplation is one of my father's talents. Once, a long time ago, my father was away on business for months we didn't know where, he came back we don't know why, he set down his case, ate some meat, drank, took a shower, drank more, settled down in his boxers and watched television.

Another time, I was thinking of adulthood as the state of complete physical and moral fulfilment, my father had been gone more than a year, he came back who knows why, he set down his case, ate some chips and garlic gratin tomatoes, he drank, took a bath, drank more and contemplated his computer.

Later, I was wondering if complete physical and moral fulfilment was within anybody's grasp, my father had gone who knows why, he came back to pick up some things, he filled two bags, he ate some royal sea bream with fennel and a tiramisu, he drank, washed his hands, drank more and contemplated his mobile phone.

A year later, I was wondering if complete physical and moral fulfilment is possible only in a society that demands complete physical and moral fulfilment, my father had come back for his things, he set down his case, he drank, he contemplated my mother, said she'd better get out fast because he was back home, he drank more, ate some cod *brandade*, raped my mother and contemplated a book.

Not every father has to match the American dream of the paternal fiction, here's the real thing.

The American father who comes back from the war and hugs you in his GI arms, the tears of joy at the airport, that's not your father.

The father who's worn your photo thin with kissing it amid desert storms, that one's not your father.

The patriot who'll bring you a souvenir from the country to show how much you mean to him, the guy who thinks that after years of absence he'll draw you back in with one commercial hook, that one might be a famous GI but he's not your father.

The father who's proud of you when he knows nothing about your life but trusts you are a good person, remember once and for all that he is not your father.

Don't trust the American fiction, fathers who aren't there don't miss anyone. Now if, one fine day, this father plays the trick of the returning warrior on you and you go along with it, if the sincerity of a father hugging you tight in order to wipe the slate clean has you in tears, you'll know you're a hopeless poet.

Sincerity is an American fiction, said my father one day he'd been drinking.

Lesson two: *Poets, don't look for sincerity in poetry; there's nothing in this American sentiment that's worth saving.*

Genuinely every time I've meant to be sincere, I've done nothing at all but believe in what I believed since me and society and society and me, as if society and I were birds of a feather. I sincerely believed in sincerity, sincere poetry ought to come from the heart, my heart was where I tapped into the goodness that was beautiful, the beauty that was true, the truth of nature and a somewhat traditional nature it was. I left no country stone unturned, no ear of wheat, no oats or wayside flowers or little birds, I wanted all of creation to be sincere, what a fucking farce. I'd even tried to get myself a university education so as to have a degree that would guarantee State-approved sincerity, I sincerely wanted to achieve sincerity, the American kind, as they're reputed to be the sincerest of all the nations. I've hung around a free verse undergrad class on Whitman and Ginsberg, taught by a professor who spoke English with the accent of French Literature, which opened strange perspectives and closed quite a few others; Whitman had become Saint Whitman and Ginsberg Saint Ginsberg, holy holy holy, but I mainly realized that Whitman and Ginsberg were nuts, each in his own way, and I did consider the question of illegal substances.

"Is that all you managed to do at uni—you started smoking?"
"That at least, Papa."

"And I draw to your attention that the Earth is the only suicidal planet in the galaxy, perhaps even in the entire Universe."

"I don't see the connection."

"There isn't one. I'm telling you anyway."

I started to batter my braincells over planetary movement, what does Ginsberg's sincerity mean if you don't understand *the whole boatload of sensitive bullshit*, Whitman's sincerity when you don't understand the Earth nor any of its satellites, when you can't even say the word Earth without blushing in shame, *Have you reckoned the earth much?* How can you study when you don't know the first thing about life, *Have you felt so proud to get at the meaning of the poems?* And you hardly know how to boil an egg.

3

Between November and March, was it December, the good city of Lyon's regular Festival of Lights was off the agenda, that was for sure, I didn't give a fuck, the leaves were dead and the flowers ugly, the Quais de Saône market was staked out by paratroopers, I was in a fug over finding work so I'd have a profession because, as they say, jobs are such reptilian creatures, they've none of life's warm-blooded features, they truly are alien to the wide range of our aspirations. I'd looked through the classifieds for poets wanted, I'd had this idea of a job in nothing supervised by no one that I felt corresponded with a lack of profile that was difficult to encapsulate in a list of skills; under "poet" I found a job for an e-learning technical editor for a leading industrial company in its sector and ads written in advertising couplets for becoming human with clear sight and a sense of security mid-desert, such as: *I come from afar and I'll go far*

I want to forge ahead to make sure liberty never takes a
backward step
I shall develop my skills
I hope to be a breath of fresh air after the storm
I'm happy to be in the service of other humans
I shall act with the will to win

With the army embarked on a nationwide campaign, that's 15,000 jobs for site cleaners, sports instructors, weapons training, implementation workshops, equipment maintenance and operational activities. Far from being inaccessible, still the training maintains a few prerequisites:

We are seeking
Fairly
Mature
Candidates
Motivated young people who have
Both
Stamina and
Courage
Show reasonable independence of spirit
And a degree of toughness
In order to cope with
Stress
As well as fatigue

On the banks of the Saône and in our state of emergency, strolling as best I could among the troops I wasn't overthinking it, saying to myself Don't think about it, saying without thinking Keep going, keep on strolling, thinking while strolling The state we're in isn't due to emergency, thinking without saying to myself and all the while strolling This hardy breed of army bloods are young and motivated, was saying while continuing to stroll These young motivated kids are armed, continuing to stroll thinking They've had lessons in handling weapons, assembly and disassembly, safety regulations but also shooting practice, saying to myself Four of them, picturing them while strolling without thinking about it Of the four, only one motivated young man need panic at a bird flying over for the brave rugged soldier trained to handle weapons to start firing and for the other three mature and hardy independents to start firing too in kneejerk sympathy or an overbearing desire to serve the nation, yet I read a survey or somesuch in the good city of Lyon's *Le Progrès* that showed objectively the effectiveness of soldiers in urban settings, and indeed 80% of residents are reassured by the presence of soldiers marching nicely through the streets of the peninsula with machine guns. *Never before has there been an age in which the state has pursued the protection of its citizens so assiduously with charitable intentions that surely deserve to be better appreciated.*

"Who's that from?"
"That's Karl Kraus, Papa."

From the roof of the Fourvière basilica, my father trained his telescope at the shapely wake of a Boston Whaler 350 Outrage captained by the nephew of the CEO of the surveillance company post-crackdown on the good city of Lyon's street market.

"Are you reading Karl Kraus?"
"I've begun to. Do you know Kraus?"
"Of course I do, I've read and reread him, but that's not the problem."
"What problem, Papa?"

He extended a telephoto lens and machine-gunned through a flock of ducks, black against the water.

"You think Karl Kraus will help you find a job?"

My father climbed back into his helicopter, he was heading out to fly over the vale of chemistry and make sure the flues were indeed belching their smoke and flame as they ought upon all the usual suspects, the clouds making a light haze i.e., nothing to worry about. I went on stretching my legs in the months between the Paris and the Nice attacks, I was looking for a way of not thinking about looking for work so I wouldn't have to look for it and fill my head with rubbish, I rummaged through the crates of good old literature, behind some *Temps modernes* there was poetry, Hölderlin was wondering what the point of poets was in these troubled times, a fine question, and Rilke was recommending deep inner solitude for me and to retreat inside myself and not see anyone and be alone as a child, another fine idea; next to them were the Zolas and the Victor Hugos and beneath them, in a cardboard box on the ground with the *Mickey Mouse* and *Life* magazines and other American excesses, *Howl and Other Poems*, I'd studied it in college but hadn't understood a thing because of Literature, it was a 1956 edition, my father said it was worth a fortune and also quite a bit more than that, but what is worth, is it the authenticity, the rarity, the equilibrium price or the outcome of productive work, I said go to hell, I had no intention of making a foray into his philosophy, I zipped the book inside my jacket, assumed a distracted look and slipped away off, down below, on the riverbank. I started to read "In Back of the Real" in Ginsberg's language.

railroad yard in San Jose
I wandered desolate
in front of a tank factory

and sat on a bench
near the switchman's shack.

I decided there was no sincerity to be found in railroads or in tank factories or in benches or shacks, nor even in switchmen; that you couldn't give a damn whether the railroad, the tank factory, the bench and shack and switchman were sincere, nor know if Ginsberg was sincere when he wrote railroad, tank factory, bench, shack and even switchman, nor whether San Jose hadn't come from Ginsberg's heart, hadn't come from him in sincerity but that San Jose was no more or less than San Jose and all that went with that, e.g., a railroad and a tank factory. I pictured Ginsberg wandering or roaming or tramping desolate or ruined in front of the tank factory, poet or not, the war machine on his back and a single yellow flower like the ones around here which shoot up their determination until they shatter the cement of the steps down to the boats.

I watched the water flow south and the swans driven by their insignificance, deaf and blind to the basic shapes of the food-processing industry, ignorant that they, poor sods, were beholden to market price variation over the kilo of feathers and to the planned obsolescence of ornamental fowls. The day swans are personally concerned about famine in the world they will swan about less, but as long as they're not force-feeding themselves or raising themselves free-range or in batteries and then self-electrocuting or cutting their own throats and auto-plucking and chopping themselves into thighs or nuggets, they'll go on showing off their little number in back of the real, Fuck you swans, I shouted at them in Ginsberg's language, they chortled among themselves in swan language, we were practically enemies when they made lift-off from the water, with their wings fanned right out, waddling on their webbed feet, apparently modeling the culture of nature for humanity's heritage. *Oh—swans!* That was some demented old crackpots traveling down on a cruise in an organised group, pocketing the free show of this ballet on the Saône like a well-deserved payback for consumer credits, for space odysseys, for washing machines and frozen meals, old bastards, pray for a health insurance card and the cost of your funeral and dig into red meat as often as you like. And then hell broke loose right over my head.

Someone jumped down from the street onto the riverbank, about three meters down, cops from the special forces jumped down after him, the first one locked him in a krav maga neck hold, he was also seasoned in the art of tonfa and equipped with technical mastery of professional intervention methods as well as in defense and interrogation, having completed training programs designed to create the total fighter, able to react efficiently in the most stressful conditions with decisiveness and aggression proportionate to the situation at hand. Another cop dragged the guy towards the landing steps and put his knee across his windpipe, a third jammed his SP2022 against his forehead, each of them able to take pleasure in the Sig Sauer designed in Switzerland by SIG and manufactured by Sauer in Germany, this weapon is recognized in all the countries that agree on human rights and even beyond for its simultaneously Swiss and German qualities, that's why the SP2022 is the standard service weapon currently used by the French national police force, by the Gendarmerie and the frontier guards. If you want to know, superior quality materials, including tempered steel, carbon steel and special barrel steel, are used to resist corrosion; the trigger guard, it's worth noting, has a serrated finger-rest to provide better shot control and the grips have been refined for better purchase in-hand and for rapid unholstering, an appreciable improvement. The load indicator offers both tactile and visual oversight of cartridge-loading while other noteworthy special features include easy disassembly for cleaning and maintenance of the weapon; in short, superior quality and reliability are what make SIG Sauers the most popular sidearms in all the armed forces; it's impossible to overstate: the SP2022 delivers optimum security, reliability and precision, etc. A fourth man joined the scene by way of the steps, he locked hand-cuffs onto the wrists of this individual of regulated ethnic profile, he was most probably unlikely to be French.

Lesson three: *Poets, write national poems—they're the securest type there is.*

I wandered without keeping track, I was wandering and smoking, smoking and wandering, I was roaming nowhere in particular and roving not knowing what to think, I was thinking about nothing, dreaming about nothing, if somewhere there's a loner blessed with an active imagination, always journeying through the great human desert, if someone is still trying to spy in modernity something beautiful that's useful to no one, tell them for me that they're in a time no pre-centenarian can understand because you can always wander, you'll only ever be a poor bastard incapable of active imagination so not even a poet, you'll see nothing because you see what's happening and, you see, what's happening bears no relation to this modernity whose beauty will be revealed in the smog of its exhaust, in its everyday privations, in the dogs that chase their living in the soughing rain or the stinking glare of the unimportant streets, go on wander as much as you want, for poetry is dead and void. All that you can gather from your idiotic roaming is that the present is sick to the back teeth with that quip about the beauty of time i.e., curtains for half your poem in progress, and besides, during the time you're wandering in this poetic abyss, Baudelaire and Verlaine and Rimbaud, those illustrious consumers of hovering products, are just about good for getting yourself locked into school programs or to be exchanged on the European market of first year Literature for credits such a fucking farce.

Junkies are the exception that confirms the rule, said my father one day when he'd been drinking.

Late afternoon and I thought about going home, I walked towards my place in a state of emergency, I needed to piss, I pissed without wandering, I conjugated to wander in the past perfect with uncertainty about the employment of the future, even having stopped wandering I couldn't see myself working now, and never even, never, I took my clothes off, I wanted to be naked to shed the showy signs of civility, fucking farce, naked the human appears an ape, seen within its natural state, I looked at my state in the bathroom mirror and saw that my skin had no colour and my reflection hadn't either, no data, I'd had to go back to this, the color you see or the one you don't have so then I put on Tupac, "Never Had a Friend Like Me" and "Smoke Weed All Day," and I smoked until a crow appeared unsummoned and I sensed my beetroot field of ideas where the clouds' shadows pool over land-scapes criss-crossed by wolves on the loose from the food chain or something like that, there was just a pot of jam and an old banana. You could make yourself a baby purée with those, which takes me back to think-ing about my mother who's been dead a good while already, so that explains that. I opened the computer and ate my purée while reading what I could find on police weaponry. Then I threw up the sincere poetry along with the purée and went to lie down with a beer and a plan to wallow in despair, listening to *Lonely, lonely, lonely, lonely eyes, / lonely face, lonely lonely in your place* because really, and precisely if you strip back to brass tacks, it appears that we are unspeakably alone and *Way down in the hole* because of what's going on right behind you and that it'd be better if you could see, *Well I beg your pardon*, I'll have to straighten out and get a job, I wanted to defang this idea of a job but the idea keeps biting back, you gotta do it, that's all, as people do with work, they do it, but how when you don't have time because of all the time that passes and the days that are measured out? Because if you have a job, I mean a real job, I mean a State-sanctioned job, be aware that you're made available, that you will con-form and that you're not free, which is what a long

poem entitled "Law no. 2016-1088" says, of which a
few lines will be enough for you to get the gist:

Effectively the duration of the work is the time
During which
The employee is
Available to the employer and
Compliant with their instructions
Without being able
Freely
To go about
Their personal
Affairs.

I was aware of the immorality of a time that might
suspend its flight while others are rising early to get to
work, I knew perfectly well that an argument of the
too old to lose it, too young to choose it type was worth-
less from the standpoint of how lucky we are when
we have a future. I have a future thanks to the past, a
past glorious with my father's glory, his tragic ancestor being author to the first great deed and followed
by many others, to list them milk powdered, cartoned
and tubed, chocolate dark, white, milk or with hazel-
nuts, with whatever you fancy, in tablets, bars or Easter
rabbits, coffee ground then freeze-dried, then encap-
sulated, and then the climate started heating up, the

market for thirst and the buying-up of water sources like so many gold mines, there you have a few of the feats that illustrate this steady lineage of protestant ethics and capitalism to which I belong though I never asked to, which spreads its plastic bottles everywhere and its iron in the soul.

The iron in the soul is perhaps the flipside of the flower in the gun, it's the mist rising from the graveyards of the Somme and the Meuse, from the silence of the earth and the industry of war. *You are going to fight*, one poet said, I remember because of college, another went to war; he said *I have a sense of reality, me, the poet. I've acted. I've killed. Like one who wants to live*, they used to say that in the trenches while an inherited friend of a great-grandfather in my line of benefactors, a friend who, later, would be cordially conned by the son of the last of my father's line to which I belong, claimed the victory of the OXO cube on all fronts.

I didn't learn all of this straightaway. I had to smoke a fair bit while staring at a cubist painting, one you find online when you google *who sells soup*, for all the pixels of this great bedlam of a trench war to come back into focus, and for me to start thinking about the actions of societies and of their armies.

4

On my bed I was thinking about how I was doing, it wasn't tip-top, not far off being a clairvoyant who can't see or a princess who's never done anything but dream things up while combing her golden locks or an old man who doesn't have a single memory of his own. When you see someone, a black guy, though do I need to say it, getting punched in the chest with the full force of a cop and all his impunity then being dragged away by another who kicks him to a pulp on the riverbank pavement, you realize that all you've been able to write in your gilded youth is pure crap.

Once, was it to prove that I was of the human species despite all that past and my father's lineage, I began my biography as if I'd had a life although I still don't know what it means to have left childhood behind. Yes indeed, I wrote pages and pages of my life story, pure fakery of the real life genre, I drew myself being born into a brand-new era and I developed myself in line with the emotional attitudes of those lost causes that make you rebel, attitudes I had found in old new wave films, their words like actions and violence mixed up with love, that all added up to a real life but it was all fake. Even those 1970s films with their themes of urban loneliness and suicidal company execs, their dialogues, so stupid and so real between Romy Schneider and Michel Piccoli, for me they stuck much too closely to the stuff of life to be credible. In this biography I became someone, not a face or a type or a character but a kind of specifically social figure tied to a moment in an environment, but after a while I had to make the call between this role and the iron in the soul which really can't be ignored either, so I gave up. To become someone with a social position you probably ought to have special equipment, weapons, a shield, ear-protectors, a helmet, a bulletproof vest or a chain mail tunic.

"What were you trying to do? Write a chivalric romance?"

My father had emerged from the Hispanic region of my frontal lobe, spitting out watermelon pips at intervals while rereading chapter VI of the first volume of *Don Quixote de la Mancha*, for my father often rereads what he's never read and even books he never will read.

"Just like Esplandián, whose exploits entailed his auto-da-fé in the process of the amusing and great inquisition that the priest and the barber conducted in the library of our ingenious hidalgo, you can't hold a candle to Amadís de Gaula!"

"Do you mean my biography's just good for kindling?"

The wind rocked the made-in–Sri Lanka Yucatecan hammock suspended among the cypresses on one of the six terraces of Welles's Italian *Estate of Don Quixote*, of which the unimaginable value had gone up again following the creation of a genuine Pompeiian mosaic designed by a friend of Buren and pieced together by thirty-odd Albanian laborers at two euros an hour plus bottled water at the rate of a six-pack per week plus one coffee capsule for a productivity bonus.

"I'm just observing, broadly, that there's no point publishing measly feats of heroism when you're lucky enough to have a father as exemplary as was Amadís."
"But Papa, without wishing to annoy nor to reproach you, I don't remember your having done, I mean personally done, anything at all exemplary."
"It's enough that I exist to ensure I'll have existed and vice versa, and likewise that I become myself. That is what's exemplary. So let it be a lesson to you."

Lesson four: *Poets, do not seek out many exemplars. Just one is already too much.*

I am like my father but much less good, my father can do anything because he does nothing, while I do nothing because I don't know how to defend a person who's being crushed and dragged along the ground and kicked to a pulp with complete impunity, nor do I know how to get a job or write a CV or any biography, nor even poetry, not a single line of it. To write a single line, so it seems, you have to have looked on many cities, men and things, you have to know your animals and sense how birds fly and understand the movements little flowers make as they open in the morning, fucking farce, there are no flowers in the good city of Lyon apart from hothoused for sale elsewhere and the seeds of a few weeds that don't add up to anything, the cops trampled the one that grew in back of the real and it didn't even emit the shriek of a beauty being crushed, *O pain of the flowers in the dark air*—there, I've said it, the flowers are dying, it hurts, fine, but then we should also talk about the bees and the rhinos and the orangutans which I consider like brothers and about the tigers and the gnus and all that agonize under this dying sun, then your poetry could indeed be an ecological disaster and so an entirely un-natural calamity, but all right, conceding that there are

still a few birds in flight for us to sense, I can already
hear my father: If that's what you're up to, sensing
birds, in this era of technological evolution and extremely serious threats, but what was he on about, was
it war or the global climate? That was in November, I
remember because my father was in Arizona to watch
the supermoon above Canyon Lake, and he'd sent me
a text: *Lol nt worth worrying re nature and all small tings
no1 crs, or sthing u cant describe yrself bc huge, dont stress
the Paris conf will sort it all Papa w luv.* Two minutes later
another text: *U really think ull change sthing by tkg re
birds compared to probs of glob warming? dont forget planes
count 4 8% of glob emissions. Papa kisses.* Thirty seconds
later I received a pic of the supermoon with a plane
flying across it, actually that's what I'd have liked, to
receive a supermoon with a plane and messages of en-
couragement for atmospheric improvement, all signed
off Papa, a kind of long-distance connection. Sometimes I think maybe he's dead, to reassure myself, or
instead I wonder if he's doing it absent-father style so
that I can't manage without his advice but, shit, after all, what's he doing—him, my father—to save the
planet?

"I'm winning a round against the enemies of peace thanks
to an international intervention team made up of valiant
and courageous heroes from every corner of the world."

"Papa, it's a computer game."

"So what?"

"Computer games are no more than a way of using up unused brain time. Papa, you said it yourself one day when you'd been drinking."

My father smiled just then in a manner authorized by the code of his tragic ancestor's smile. He really wants me to send him a few heckles soon as he's managed to blow up some enemies of Overwatch.

"Do you even know what the brain is? Sometimes I wonder."

"The brain, Papa?"

"The brain is a muscle. It needs to be trained. Computer games are like a workout for it. So let that be a lesson."

Pointless telling my father that the brain isn't a muscle, he's immune to that kind of detail, he adapts science to explain his principles, it's a fairly widespread teaching technique which demonstrates the value of scientific knowledge; my father is a font of science, he can deliver a lecture on the brain to a neurologist who'll prefer to hear his bullshit out than risk making him lose face, my father never loses face in the face of science.

"But Papa, how can I play when you're telling me to look for work?"

"You have an excessively limited understanding of the actor in the system. In this war, which began some few years ago, we are all aware that we need time, and that patience is every bit as necessary as the endurance and fierceness with which we will fight."

"You're talking nonsense, Papa."
"Maybe, but it's a quotation from our president."

I agree with my father up to a point; it's better to have fun saving the world than to attract the ire of the good city of Lyon. When you play it seems your ideal of a self becomes an ideal self, so you don't need to wait to become ideal one far-off future day, you idealize yourself right away thanks to a life drive that's balanced with the death drive you find in the drive to play the game; I learned this when I set these Freudian drives that you find all over the place alongside Schiller's, which I downloaded as a gesture to my mother, who was reading his *Letters* in the hospital where she died quite a few years ago, so that explains that.

I admit that this rapprochement of Schiller and Freud's different drives is an entirely personal piece of DIY

and a kind of practical theory in this virtual world,
but you can use it to get over what's to come in time
by playing obsessively, and this was working quite
well for me, I had good firepower, I was killing easily
like someone who's going to survive, there were even
moments when I'd accumulated so many life points I
could have gone on for centuries without worrying
about the snipers that come at you out of the wood-
work, it helped me unwind as my mother would have
said if she'd been allowed to speak but she's been dead
a while, so that explains that. Really, all you need to
know is that the ideal self is always a mix of power in
action and mild revulsion that's more or less bearable.
I played I played and then I stopped, after a stint of
killing and dying you get more and more of the mild
revulsion, your father can remind you about the gran-
deur of heroism all he likes, one day you'll wonder
why keep on living and killing and dying and all that
follows and you go out in the rain or the clouds or
whatever, you're wakened by the weather of a parallel
world in motion, you decide that the game's design-
ers must be somewhere in this parallel world drinking
bottled water and looking out for everything they can
put towards building a decent place where all play-
ers can enjoy being sharpshooters, and at once you're
disarmed. Between one attack and the next your conscience suddenly awakes due to a need for the world

to be beautiful or at least kinder, then you imagine the true stories lived by real people, you think of the victims of all that isn't beautiful and really not kind, like war and hatred, at the time I was looking for a peaceful solution between my internal conflicts and global conflicts the like of Syria, was it in March, I remember a law was going to let the government gather data about the geopolitical and strategic stakes as well as the threats and risks that could affect national life due to remote interceptions and setting up mikes and cameras and cooperation with access-providers, search engines and social networks. That didn't change anything for me as I was already under surveillance by my superego of a father, innocence must always be proven to an authority, but I wanted to show my collective conscience so I launched into engagements intending to articulate a truth about humanity which implicates us with our human nature, these were entirely fictional ideas that I could fill today's world with its humanitarian tragedies, it was making me weep with pro-African empathy, with seagoing grief, with migratory odysseys, health crises, universal rights, with the fight against hunger and thirst in the world, because despite technological developments and the extreme seriousness of the looming threats we are still human therefore full of humanity, as humans are bound to appear, humanity at its best and in all its glory, fucking farce, human misery has dumped me with a cold that's lasted for days, my father had some fun with it, he wouldn't stop reminding me that like him I belonged, oh yes, to that agri-food lineage, that I'd therefore never had the merest experience of hunger or thirst so what made me someone who could talk about either without being ridiculous or even becoming frankly appalling? Because we ought to know if it's really serious, all these lyrical tirades about the hunger and the thirst and about humanity when you come from an agri-food line of business and have all you need to be yourself, whatever the situation in northern Mali or South Sudan, doubtless in our Olympian way. Would you die if you were banned from writing? Hm? Would you die of it?

I said no. Mustn't give people too much shit.

Lesson five: *Poets, if you are banned from writing, try first to realize this.*

Real life stories full to the gills with humanity have drained out of my head, and besides I can't write a complete story anymore, I mean an old-school one, with its end that's been once around the block and all that goes with that. I did it just the once and the story wasn't my own but that of the sister-in-law of an aged aunt of my father; it sold very well in the supermarkets, it's a *thickwit novel*, that's what I call it, which allows me to live without shame and which I signed with a name I found on that mashed potato that comes in packets. Apart from this youthful error which gives pause though I don't know what about, according to my meager experience and humble opinion, history never gets all the way around anywhere and you can never tell how it'll end. Even poetry with its strophes all aligned like little coffins for the Springtime of the Poets looks a lot like a good slice of the culture sector with the criteria barriers and hoops to jump through for security, fucking farce.

The culture sector is a graveyard for the soul's repose, said my father one day he'd been drinking.

In order to find non-culture sector poetry, I went browsing among forums with not a single word about it, nothing on culture or springtime or anything we know to be of public utility; I particularly liked the site feminin.com, a forum specializing in humanity without criteria or hoops, for example Silv, not their real name, is writing to someone who, it seems, has had "intimate health problems":

Don't worry Me, three years ago, I reported my former step-dad for rape and unwanted touching. The facts went back that time was five years ago already. When I reported him, I didn't have any evidence either, but I had my word against his. Some policemen listened to me and some shrinks, cos they saw I was traumatized. When he was arrested, he denied it (like everyone does), but the cops didn't let go, they even got him to admit it (after 2 days . . .). And then they worked out he's tried to rape his own sister!!! I was really scared in court, I hadn't seen that monster for so many years and when I saw him I couldn't stop crying. I was scared too, whether they would believe me or whether justice wouldn't be done. But justice was done!!! He went down for 10-15 years. I also thought it was a lost cause but see, there is justice out there . . . Be brave and go report him, and speak up for your half sister too, she'll make one more witness on your side. Good luck, I'm rooting for you. If you wanna talk about it again, Im here.

No one can offer advice or help you, it seems, if your poetry is gunning for perfection but if your words are all joined up with spelling mistakes and lay no claim to a life of their own, it's as if they begin to get things moving, as if at once vulnerability became the actual source of a supreme beauty, was what I thought reading this message which hit right to the heart of my soul and the iron in it.

Apparently our Silv had been lucky, for most rapes it's worth saying that the police are not so soft on the victims, their mission is to ensure the safety of the people, goods and institutions, this is why the police protect love and passion and the whole bag of tricks that favors gamboling on the beach and rolling in the grass, and kisses and hugs like crazies in front of sunsets, fucking farce. I can't say I've understood everything about love or even about passion but it seems to me that the rape report and the image of love make up one single conception of the safety of people, goods and institutions. You might as well say that mere freedom doesn't carry much weight, contrary to what my mother used to hold, but she's been dead a good while, so that explains that.

Lesson six: *Poets, write love poems, if you wish, in full freedom and without wondering if it's too difficult.*

I'm not about to lay waste to love in its vastness thanks to a notion of sunsets going with sexual abuse, I concede all that but it's not the whole story. I think it's possible to love without security a person without goods or institutions and that that person can love with real freedom; then love would really be quite bearable. Quite bearable. I smoked without overdoing it and I put Tom Waits and Tupac on about a hundred times and then nothing at all, I stared at the ceiling until the garbage trucks started, metropolitan hygiene is these days a requirement of populations anxious for their living standards which justifies turning to a specialist company, Veolia, Victory at dawn, the birds, a fucking farce.

I think you might say I was in something of a depression.

5

I must have spent months after that reading Klemperer and Kraus while eating bananas and rereading Klemperer while smoking fairly continuously. I was getting to grips with Nazism because of Fascism and with Fascism because of this national mood, with vocabulary modifications and new approaches, as if all the hatreds that had been suppressed had the right to come out without shame or reproach. I admit I was reading Klemperer to amplify it all, because the survival of a Jewish philologist under the Third Reich remains incomparably more dreadful than that of a nobody, even one in a state of emergency in the good city of Lyon; winter was spreading its fine-grained fog, obviously it wasn't a great idea to go for a walk wearing a beard or a headscarf or to have the look of a regulated ethnic profile, but people really seemed happy to have their bags searched at the entrances to Fnac and Monoprix and to prove they were non-black and not wearing conspicuous symbols so presumably in no way non-Catholic, I sometimes went out in a conspicuous hat with a radical bobble and dark glasses, so I could check out this view, but everyone's indifferent expressions told me I had but few suspicious aspects and a fairly acceptable appearance, eccentricities being a non-conformism that's quite well integrated into the fashion world's systems, fucking farce, I was following the dogs on their forced marches, I was looking for a job in horror of finding one, I had lots to do so I went back home.

I was smoking and reading Klemperer, then reading Kraus and eating bananas, and nothing was hitting home on house arrests, police raids or enforced statelessness, nor on any of the measures in place against our threats of the utmost gravity, while reading Kraus I could see a little more clearly what can happen when freedom comes to depend upon an elevated ideal on the state-wide scale, following well-known formulae along the line of *work sets you free* and *security is the first freedom*. I could feel from the general climate that imagination was being blocked and thought paralyzed by national unity in the name of Freedom, and freedom co-opted as a reason to have no more of it. But, for all that, this wasn't Fascism and it really wasn't anything like the Third Reich here, you mustn't give people too much shit.

Why, then, when this wasn't even the Third Reich, was I still here dumbly getting bored silly by security

in the name of Freedom while panicking about looking for a job and about having one if I were ever to
find one?

"If you overthink you can't cogitate at all," my father
said one day when he'd been drinking.

Between Kraus and Klemperer there was a window
where I'd go to smoke and dream of ravaged and most
likely terrible poems that I'd write one day under the
influence of drugs, where I saw nothing emerge apart
from crows in a beetroot field and, occasionally, if I
made a real effort, a few green images, riverweed or
forests shrunk by oil-palm plantations where the great
orangutans were going to die, I saw myself among the
orangs that were utan men, people of the forest, amid
this endangered utan forest people, this utan people
that I called my people, feeding myself and them with
Kraus à la banana, reading Kraus to them, telling them
how Kraus, one of the orang-est of all these cursed
times, had felt *stunned, so to speak*, awe-stricken, so to
speak, which is to say both awed and stricken therefore unable to write in his blistering style because go
on then, my people, try writing when you've just been
knocked out, even knowing it's precisely now that we
could do with one single sentence, yes that's what we
need, a nice little orang line to tell the blistering truth

and get even with Hitler yet, despite having always written the blistering truth and exposed the servility of the approximately socialist national newspapers, he, Kraus, is awed and stricken and *knocked out, so to speak* in the very first year of the so-called thousand-year Reich, stunned in Austria by Nazism even before the Anschluss, personally awed and stricken and therefore dumb, has not the briefest sentence, no, nothing comes to him about Hitler, so he starts to write Walpurgis Night, the third one, because there've been a few Walpurgis Nights already and those were terrifying enough, from what the poets said:

These agitated ghosts, are they the poet's
Drunken thoughts, or his regret, his remorse,
Ghosts spinning to the cadence of chaos,
Or are they just dead?

"Who's that by?"
"Verlaine, Papa."
"I knew it."
"How did you know?"
"Because it's not Goethe, silly."

My father was whistling in a bath among the coconut isles, he'd set his laptop on the massage table and was also streaming a *Simpsons* episode.

Lesson seven: *Poets, try not to knock yourselves out in the name of Liberty; take a bath or watch* The Simpsons, *and if you're still no better, read page 15 of Victor Klemperer's* The Language of the Third Reich: LTI.

I couldn't stop reading and rereading page 15, at first it was okay, *Nazism permeated the flesh and blood of the people through single words, idioms and sentence structures which were imposed on them in a million repetitions and taken on board mechanically and unconsciously*, I mean Klemperer's account tallied with what we know about the Ministry of Propaganda and about Goebbels who was running it every day and every night of the apparently millenary Third Reich, such that all the Germans were indeed, as everyone knows, stupefied by this official language of Nazi propaganda which wormed its way into their flesh and blood. But it started to become problematic for my French history with what came next, because of Schiller, because of my mother who used to read Schiller, she died quite a few years ago, so that explains that. According to Klemperer, *one tends to understand Schiller's distich on a "cultivated language which writes and thinks for you" in purely aesthetic and, as it were, harmless terms. A successful verse in a "cultivated language" says nothing about the literary strengths of its author; it is not particularly difficult to give oneself the air of a writer and thinker by using a highly cultivated turn of phrase.*

I didn't understand.

I read it and reread it.

Personally, I tended to understand nothing at all about this distich of Schiller's, which I'd never read.

I didn't understand.

Still, I'd read Schiller's *Letters* which my mother was reading in the hospital where she died in her terminal stage, so that explains that.

I read and reread.

I hunted for the source of that Schiller couplet, according to my laptop it dated from 1796; you could equally say that although written in the poetic present, it's a piece of the distant past. I didn't understand why Klemperer had felt obliged to disinter an old line of Schiller's in order to write this book, *The Language of the Third Reich: LTI*, about a language that Schiller had however neither heard nor read, nor even imagined possible, given he was by then no longer of this world. I wondered.

I went to dig through the folder called "Schiller" that

I'd found on a USB key of my mother's while I was looking for her last wishes but my mother had left no wishes on this key or anywhere else. She'd surely never had the slightest intention of asking me for anything as a last wish, that's what I thought thanks to Schiller, because Schiller believed in the human capacity to create poetry or anything else without obeying one's mother's wishes, a mother's wishes played no part in Schiller's education, that my mother quite understood.

In her Schiller folder there was a great slew of stuff on Schiller and amid the chaos a doc "Poetry" and in this doc yet more Schiller chaos and finally Schiller's distich in my mother's French and Schiller's German.

Because you've fashioned a line in language duly wrought
To elevate and shape your thought, are you the poet sort?

Weil ein Vers dir gelingt in einer gebildeten Sprache,
Die für dich dichtet und denkt, glaubst du schon Dichter
zu seyn?

And then a series of lines that were perhaps just unfinished ideas:
Imagination
The strength to create images

To construct freely
A game without an aim
Building institution or
Drunken boat
Culture knows nothing about it
Humane education?

I don't follow the whole thing but this poem or what-have-you of my mother's might explain Schiller's anti-Third Reich stance, well before Klemperer was forced to focus on it, because if this *cultivated language* is none other than a *language duly wrought*, not an aimless game; if it's a collection of ready-made images, not a free construction; if it's an institution and not a drunken boat, then all poets can do now is come up with bullshit, right? That's what I'm thinking. Poetry is over when the poet can't produce *language duly wrought*. But who can? Neither poets nor anyone else, just you try it: replace the poet with someone, anyone, and the poetry with *wrought language* and the wrought language with *pre-determined forms*, the forms determined by *modes of expression*, now you understand that these modes of expression are drip-feeding their daily poison into your very way of thinking.

"That's all just claptrap."
"What, Papa?"

My father was about to leave for Notre-Dame-des-Landes or for the Larzac or Calais or the Vercors or Ventimiglia, basically for somewhere to do something.

"You can always go prattling on about language, what difference will it make?"
"I dunno, Papa."
"Saying isn't always doing, and there comes a point when doing becomes quite another thing from saying . . ."

He was packing his bag with an OS map, a compass, a Thermos, a Swiss army knife, a first-aid kit and a miner's lamp, a sleeping bag, an emergency blanket, a microfiber towel and an igloo tent, a windbreak, a balaclava, walking boots and rubber boots, carabiners, some string, a folding stool, a blow-up pillow, a mosquito net, a lunch box, tins of beans and a life jacket with a tiny whistle.

"But it is intriguing anyway, what we say, don't you think?"
"Just a bit!"

In the good city of Lyon, the Roma had vanished from Place Carnot, the Albanians had been ejected from the Kitchener Bridge, the unassorted Blacks were obediently showing their papers, which all had nothing to do with the mammoth tags along the motorways, *Death to Islam* and *Migrants out of Europe*, poisoned words of wrought language taking over as modes of expression for every person entering or leaving the city, almost nothing left to wonder about what Fascism means, just a few signs of *islamophobia*, as we say, diagnosing a rather banal problem of psychological aversion, being harmless and quite excusable between one attack and the next, there, and a few bouts of violence a little here and here, yes the minor sacrifices of a few disturbed types in the old town of Lyon, the neighbourhood listed as world heritage which is best left unvisited at any hour you're not armed up to your Viking eyebrows, but it's enough to know it and everyone does know. You can always say it's the alt-right, but if the alt-right were at all right-aligned, would there be quite so much verbiage propagated by the Chinese-whispering mainstream media?

Language does not simply write and think for me, it also increasingly dictates my feelings and governs my entire spiritual being the more unquestioningly and unconsciously I abandon myself to it. And what happens if the cultivated language is made up of poisonous elements or has been made the bearer of poisons? Klemperer's question.

What seemed to me to resonate with the Nazi period,

when poisoning the language was a full-time political propaganda activity, was the harshness of the ready-made formulae about France being united against terrorism, which encouraged the spread on the social networks, in the local and national press and from the mainstream media, all the way down to my own peers' gossip in the good city of Lyon, of howls of National favor! and of An historically Christian secular republic! and the amplification, in a form barely tempered by a limit not intended entirely to be ignored, of slogans pouring hatred on everything that can't be fixed by maintaining order and middle-class buying power.

"The middle classes? Who do you mean? Some intermediate categories? The potential consumers of coffee in capsules? A commercial target group? Is this an identifiable entity or a pure fiction of indeterminate geometry?"
"A pure fiction, Papa."
"That works better for me."

Reading and rereading Klemperer, page 15, I understood something I hadn't spotted in Kraus, the unconscious work of words and phrases, when nothing now reaches you without a world view snaking in with it such as *Weltanschauung* and the literature that still speaks and goes on speaking its cultivated language.

Lesson eight: *Poets, do not permit words to be poisoned, and stay well clear of literature.*

Even so it wasn't the Third Reich here, I ought to say that. Mustn't kick up too much shit.

6

It's true that I see fascism everywhere since there's
come to be more and more of it around, though I
don't even know what fascism means, as my father
pointed out the day after the day I said there wasn't
a lot of poetry these days. He'd landed at about five
in the morning, on waking from a dream which was
meant to lead me towards ordinary life in a standard
office in a job without a hint of originality. So it was a
labyrinth. I moved forward without dawdling. I had a
kind of hope. The hope required my sustaining some
movement in a forward direction. This movement was
no more than a mixture of courage and fear. I shivered
in my cold sweat. I was dripping and trapped like a rat.
I was afraid of courage, of what it requires. I moved
forward as one must when one is looking for a job. I
moved forward shivering and looking determined to
become everything you might wish. I was condition-
ing myself for the esteem of employment. I was gulp-
ing down drugs. I cracked open a beer. I was drinking

coffee. I ate a banana. I wonder where I'd picked up all these things. I read the CV of someone deserving of a position aloud to myself. I psyched myself up. I had to go through a series of checkpoints guarded by German shepherds. Their eyes like saucers were cameras supported in their function by a helicopter-borne device and by a task force equipped with four-wheel drive vehicles. On the walls were posted the European rights of universal man. Behind the arrow-slits, Magyar huntsmen armed with laser guns were shooting at random for a monthly salary of 150,000 forint, in other words for next to nothing. It was a mess. To get myself out of there, I had to answer to an authority, but would that be a commissioner for coal and steel, a local council employee, a benefits office inspector, an HR department or a magistrate for the good city of Lyon? I couldn't tell, in some circumstances it's impossible to differentiate one power source from another, besides that wasn't important as all I had to do was reply the way you're meant to. I had managed to regurgitate the paltry *a bird in the hand is worth two in the bush, a rolling stone gathers no moss* and *why is a raven like a writing desk*, I was moving on to *what's black and white and re(a)d all over*, little by little I was remembering most of *on Saturday and Sunday cold ovens make pastry*, ought to have been on nodding terms with *When griping grief the heart doth wound, and doleful dumps the mind oppress*, when they dropped *what is fascism* and it felt better to let the panic wake me up.

"What are you up to?"
"I'm going for a piss, Papa. What are you doing?"
"I'm planning my trip while philosophizing."

My father was sitting in his study in the right side of my brain, he was leafing through *4x4 Magazine* and, as rather often, he was polishing off a bottle of chablis or chiroubles or vosne-romanée, whichever it was he didn't look up to say that I was once more unfortunately and perhaps incurably nothing but a sad loser, for after numerous dialogues which a philosopher as wise as he was patient, he meant himself, had had the decency to entertain with said sorry loser, he meant me, I ought nonetheless and at least to have understood the following: that *fascism is a rhetorical question*, in other words and obviously a problem for sophists. Thus ought I, he arched an eyebrow, to recognise and thereupon respond to whom it may concern that *there is fascism and fascism*, considering that one should nonetheless know what one is talking about.

"And I shall add, to quote Wittgenstein, that *what can be said at all can be said clearly*, in other words, *when you've nothing to say, better shut it.*"

"You've never read Wittgenstein, Papa."

"Perhaps not, but I've an excellent understanding of the different models of Land Rover. And besides, I've read Plato."

Plato has said it all, my father said one day when he'd been drinking.

I can't read Plato because of my father who reads Plato every day, who alternates Plato and *4x4 Magazine*, who studies the pages of this repository of technical data and virile photos of off-road vehicles in mid-Moscow-Berlin rally and simultaneously pursues his version of Greek-style dialogues in which he plays the ingénu. "But what can he mean? You may know, Polemarchus, but I do not"; this is how he starts off playing the ignorant tutor, the better to demonstrate that he's always right. The effect of my father's socratic habit has always been to disqualify me on counts of error and shame, for, as I repeatedly answer "I do agree," "naturally," "so it seems," "indeed that is a consequence of this logic," of course it's always he, my father, who rejoices to see me bow to the ultimately incontrovertible: "you speak the precise truth, Socrates."

I don't doubt that in Plato we have all we need to address fascism and finally to answer the question *what is fascism*. If Plato could have written a famous socratic dialogue on fascism, he'd have kicked off something like this: Socrates arrives late due to chariot breakdown, he enquires about the latest news on world health, a Greek kid goes into the rise of fascism with him and, poised and wise in his toga, ready with his ancient socratic art of the dialectic, the great philosopher turns to Polemarchus: "Would you be so kind as to tell me, Polemarchus, what fascism is?" and, Polemarchus having quoted a sophist of his acquaintance who liked to tell Athenian citizens in the agora that "fascism is a totalitarianism," Socrates would at this juncture have played his wildcard line, "But what can he mean? Perhaps you know, Polemarchus, but I do not," and would in the end through a series of questions have led him to acknowledge that totalitarianism is not a fundamental truth but the issue of a mistaken concept of the world as divided in two by the Cold War. Veering off-topic into the connections between beauty, goodness and truth within the plurality of things in existence, via many *I grant you*s, *certainly*s and *indeed it appears*, Polemarchus would finally have been obliged unconditionally to bow to the ultimate conclusion: "You speak the perfect truth, Socrates." And thus the cookie would have crumbled.

What is fascism? is a question my superego of a father faces with a platonic tint to his shades, to make me admit that, viewed as totalitarianism, fascism has nothing to do with true meaning and that I'm still talking without actually saying anything as Wittgenstein would easily have shown him had my father read any.

That night I couldn't face the final conclusion as expected by my father. I left him alone with his magazine and his contemplation of the Moscow-Berlin rally. I hadn't the courage to talk to him about Kraus and Klemperer, neither of whom had ever said 'there is fascism and fascism" but who had set to work describing the Nazism they knew from first-hand experience having seen it destroy language and humanity wholesale, starting with children's minds, to ensure that our future's future prospects looked bleak indeed.

From day one we stuff children's heads with a stack of nonsense, said my father one day he'd been drinking.

Lesson nine: *Poets, if you're in a prison where the walls block out all the world's noise, do not rely on your childhood alone to get you out of there.*

It's through Kraus and Klemperer that we can understand what fascism is in its general sense, not only the Italian kind, and what it has become since the Reich's thousand years were buried beneath millions of corpses. Because even if there are indeed "fascism and fascism" and even if Nazism and fascism form two different regimes, fascists still refer to Nazism as the most successful exemplar of the approach that they admire. Thus the good city of Lyon's fascists, like fascists everywhere, adore the Nazis who in turn venerate Hitler whom they call the Führer. There is, in our good city of Lyon, this love for the Führer Hitler which comes via the Nazis and bypasses the comprehension of the forces of law and order.

7

So I wasn't feeling any better. On the contrary, on this particular diet of Klemperer and Kraus à la banana split, I was surely suffering a number of deficiencies, of the emotions, perhaps, and certainly of joy. Winter was over. My father had gone. I mean he'd been away for a while, probably to see a friend, probably someone I didn't know, who was probably in a terrible state, who probably needed his help, because this friend probably had an awfully sick girlfriend, who my father was visiting every day in a probable hospital, probably in the palliative care phase, thus he was probably passing the hours by holding the hand of the probable girlfriend of this probable friend; my father is sensitive and kind to others.

"You weren't there when I needed you, Papa."
"When?"
"I could've croaked."
"Are you alive now?"

"Yes."

"So what's the problem?"

I was trying not to think about looking for work, which is immoral, I wasn't hoping to earn a living, which is pretty unusual, I couldn't have cared less about the cash, which is reckless in these times of very grave threats, but I was scraping a living already, which was repugnant, on the minuscule royalties from a *thickwit novel*, which is scandalous, that I'd created from the stories of a brilliant and brittle grand dame of theater, survivor of a romance full of stereotypes, which makes you think though I don't know what about. When I say *thickwit novel,* it's not that I don't respect my great actress who had nothing to do with it, no it's that *the novel* is thickwitted, for as far as I know it's still on the supermarket shelves with the following thickwit title: *But Can You Not Understand That Life is Too Short.* It's an alexandrine, the classical dodecasyllabic line. I should add that the title came from the editor, a certain Zozo who'd had the idea of copying the idea from a hotshot professor who sells very well indeed, in order to develop an ambitious yet broadly appealing collection in which the marketing patter would join the highly literary aims of making *cultivated language* accessible to the greatest number of consumers, which required that I insert myself into this poignant and banal tale filled with universal feelings, a few flurries of twelve-syllable lines, that is a few sets of six times two, actually:

Thus the days went by in deeply felt emotions,
She looked down at her hands, how was it she could have
Allowed herself to play out this criminal role?
And nonetheless within her heart there throbbed a hope, etc,
etc.

Truly pure bollocks. But this *thickwit novel* enables me to eat and pay my rent without asking my father or anyone else for anything.

If I'm bringing my *thickwit novel* in at this point, it's solely to show that there is no financial dependency whatsoever between my father and me. Money problems are invisible to my father, who has it, money I mean; and same with me, in that I don't give a shit, insofar as that's possible. In a way, *But Can You Not Understand That Life is Too Short* is a kind of ode to money which doesn't apply to those who have it or to those who don't give a shit as much as possible. *But Can You Not Understand That Life is Too Short* has allowed me to stay at home and grow ever more anxious about finding work even while sweetly dreaming of poetry although this wasn't even the Third Reich nor even fascism, one still mustn't kick up too much shit.

Of course, in these extremely serious times, my guilt complex was at peak performance. Each day I spent thinking about fascism and poetry while not giving a shit about everything, when there was even meant to be a law making work even less enjoyable, plunged me deeper into the torments of the price to be paid by those who continued to buy *But Can You Not Understand That Life is Too Short* in supermarkets with a price tag of €16 or, in recent months, in the mass-market edition, at €7.

Lesson ten: *Poets, forget the classical meters, except if it's to keep you above the breadline.*

Alexandrines sell by the dozen, said my father one day when he'd been drinking.

For food I went to the Arab cornershop. I always bought the same things, not Arabic biscuits or Arabic veg or Arabic tins of sardines but Arabic coffee and Arabic bananas, the Arab fed me without asking anything of me, the more I fed myself from the Arab cornershop the more I grew capable of feeling alive. One evening it was strange, I felt alive, I felt like talking, I started with the origin of French Arabic bananas from Martinique; the Arab asked if Martinique was a region or an overseas department, I said both, he didn't reply, I added that the Martinican bananas were outsize bananas because the use of chemical treatments is enabling the continued destruction of the land and seas, he asked will that be all? No there was the Arabic coffee from Colombia produced by fair-trade processes, I told him I was wondering how exploitation without exploitation could have become a sales hook, he had no idea, this aspect of the business was beyond him, me too, I said, after a certain point I didn't get it, yet I often go back to agri-food questions because of my father and his family line, though the more I think about it the less I see a way through it, I often dream of having my very own garden but that's utopian; I have no land, he said me neither, I said, but it looks as though there is some on top of Perrache station with tomato plants and city radishes, not a Voltairean thing but a political field for direct action, it was a student who told me about it before the attacks, we were on a bench under the trees at Carnot, behind the barrier for the ceremony of 8 May 1945, when Indochina vets used to hold forth about all the deaths under the tricolour banner, he was studying biology but not in order to work in labs as the ideology of success at any cost would have it, he wanted to become an anti-agriculture market gardener, he imagined the Revolution arriving via culture, announcing that the Pilat's small producers' seasonal spirit would

soon descend to transform the town into an agri-
cultural "commune"; I would see, one day, how the
short circuits would short-circuit the multinationals,
everything would change without pissing around with
armed struggle, with nothing but a garden on top of
a train station where wild animals beyond anyone's
ken had already taken up residence, he listed seven-
teen species of bird, not counting the mice, slugs and
beetles, talk about a bestiary, fucking farce, but it felt
good to talk it through while the Arab's radio went
on about a demo against the new employment law as
well as against the extremely serious threats. The Arab
scanned my items, he asked for €5.70, then he said I'm
not Arabic. I said I know but I hadn't known. He said
Arabic is a language. I said I know. He said I'm open
till midnight, I know the stars. He said, the science of
the stars doesn't belong to anyone. I said, of course.
He said I've counted the stars of the united Americas
and European states, he said I'm international and I
tell each star to go to hell by name.

This was the beginning of "Arabic," a text I wrote
without sincerity, as if everything went straight from
the Arab and back to the Arab and I couldn't say anything more real while knowing nothing of the truth.
The Arab had me write "Arabic" although I don't
know Arabic, through my ignorance of Arabic this
"Arabic" begins. I can't say I knew what I was doing

writing "Arabic," and anyway I hadn't meant to write poetry, sincere or otherwise, you can't say how or why but there, all at once you're not relying on anything, not on political culture or on bottled water, you say everything without knowing, there's no one left to keep you safe, for in the end, and precisely where it counts, we are inexpressibly several, so you start thinking and talking beyond the pale of your *cultivated language*, you don't know what you're doing, you find a way of experiencing ideas without their being effective.

"That doesn't mean a thing."
"I know, Papa."
"Bottled water—it's ridiculous."
"Yes, Papa."

"Inexpressibly several?"

"What, Papa?"
"Forgive me, that's genuinely ludicrous."

"But you rely on bottled water like everybody else."
"I know."
"Though you don't look like it."

"Ineffective ideas—there I follow you."
"Get off my case, Papa."

My father was right. At the same time, he was becoming a real pain in the backside.

8

My ineffective ideas were destined for failure. You can succeed, that's what I was thinking to encourage myself along this route without a future, but I wouldn't be able to succeed without screwing up because all success derives from the effectiveness of my father's ancestors' agri-food business to which I belong although I never asked to.

The rout of ineffectiveness is an agro-alimentary success, my father said one day when he'd been drinking.

Everything contributes to the effectiveness of the agri-food business, that's the truth. Any job in the naval dockyards or in steel or the service industry or in administration or banking or business or education or culture is always *in fine* in the service of the agri-food business; even the production of a novel as idiotic as *But Can You Not Understand That Life is Too Short* is *in fine* an agro-alimentary triumph by extension of the supermarket aisles dedicated to the sector. Still, job losses and breaks in production are likewise profitable for our agri-food business. Just as all production or work, and all breaks in production and cuts to jobs, whether agri-jobs or not, necessarily connect you, through the food chain, to the agri-food sector, so my ineffective ideas were destined to swirl among thousands of statements broadly about the world and its state of emergency due to the extremely critical threats facing it, without having the least effect on employment and its devastations nor on the courses of action and obligations of my father's sector to which I belong.

Fuck this for a farce, it was March.

I felt good in March. Despite global warming, air pollution, the nuclear danger, over-exploitation of the land and seas, species extinction and extremely grave planetary threats, between one attack and the next I would repeat lines that started with *you'll see one of these days* and finished with *we shall fight them in the streets*, after the song of a poet led by luck and long since vanished but which could still be heard echoing through the backstreets of Les Pentes and on Radio Canut despite the good city of Lyon's CCTV; from the first bright days of the eternal return there'd been a mood of stairways in the rain, of painting on the

walls and of dogs without masters, it was a natural im-
pulse which explodes at and against everything, which
I could feel coming in with the social movements and
the returning birds.

Those birds had cranked up their lousy music again
but I couldn't give a toss even if they were musicians
or representatives of a quaint revival or if like every
year they were obliged to play airborne extras for the
heavenly beauty or the liberal arts or this, that or the
other, no, what seemed favorable to poetry was that
they took on board their own avian viewpoints by
sharing independent ideas that would never fly. And
the social movements were looking quite promising.

I'd seen them coming with *that expression popularized
by a journo-school sociology beholden to Grub Street*, as my
father observed from his hot-air balloon between the
police copters, but it was fine by me. They were *movements*, which does no harm when you haven't left your
domicile for the entire winter without even having
been under house arrest, and they were *social*, so might
be able to winkle me out of a confinement spent reading Klemperer and Kraus while smoking bananas, for
we were many, as the good city of Lyon's *Le Progrès*
would have to admit in a few lines of verse that was
blank if not free:

Many thousands of people
7,000 according to the mayor's office
Marched on Wednesday afternoon
Through the streets of Lyon
Under a variety of banners
Protesting against the proposed workers' rights reform bill

Next morning I was still staring at beetroot in a field of crows and running through metaphors of clouds over forests and plains, but what I saw was not so lovely a scene as to demand I shape an apologia for the smoke and its inspirations, it was more a case of desperation and always over the same thing, after a time spent living with your own images they get mixed up with the iron in your soul, fucking farce, I wanted to go and see what might kick off despite the threats of extreme severity, the times were auspicious for my social awakening, I hunted for my hat with the radical bobble, I found the perfect color raincoat, I considered a social model, but as I couldn't decide on one I felt more like roaming under the rubric of an unemployee, it'd make a change from the poets, the city was more immense, the peddlers of ugly art had shut up shop, Bellecour was in the West, the king's horse was wet through, the red cobbles of the Place were sticking to its hooves, in front of the Café de France and the HSBC rows of riot police were awaiting their moment for self-expression, the high-school students had crossed the sacred district of families united by marriage shouting *Ah-, Anti-, Anti-capitalist* and the unionists were surging in via Perrache and La Guillotière singing realist songs claiming that *in the streets is where it all goes down,* everyone stopped for a moment in the rain, I wasn't cold either, I was thinking about love, I don't know why I thought there must be someone among us with whom it could happen for me, someone also feeling that work is a wicked law and that education for freedom should still be the top priority, as Schiller had said through my mother's life, so that explains that, someone or no one, just one perhaps, that one or someone, she and I, he and I, *we would look at each other and smile,* it was a sweet notion of love to entertain but lasting a mere instant, at Jean-Macé the demonstration took off again, running down the side streets and belting out the chants at the Place du Pont in memory of the Lyon Commune uprising or in memory of nothing, back at Bellecour there were water cannons firing in the rain and a republican division in full security formation, security being the first of the freedoms, according to the Minister of the Interior, for you have to work, everyone was running and crying because of the tear gas, for you are at the employer's disposal and must adhere to their orders, rubber bullets were streaking towards legs and bellies because you mustn't go freely about your own affairs, someone seized my arm and pulled me behind the newspaper kiosk, I waited there, I wanted to throw up, there were four or five of us grieflessly crying because it was spring. One of us or someone said get moving, she began to run towards Antonin-Poncet, I ran with her or was it him, I can't remember why I had to cover my head with my arms, if it was the tonfas or the weaponized de-kettling grenades, she had vanished between the columns of the Armenian memorial where the forces of law and order in training could put their guerrilla mode to the test because security is the first freedom, right, said someone, I gotta go, me too I said, and she went off towards the rue de la Ré, it was still raining, I wasn't crying now, I put my fists in my mac pockets, on rue de la Charité I could hear culture streaming from the windows, it sounded like a Mozart sonata.

9

I hung my clothes out to dry, showered then wandered around naked eating a banana, I tidied everything away as if someone might drop by to see me, I even considered separating day from night by making my bed but the doorbell rang, I put my sheet on like a toga and went to answer the door, it was some vendors of good news, Christ had been resuscitated in order to save us from IVF and surrogacy should that interest me, I said I was more of the Hellenistic tendency and favored a broadly LGBTQ angle, they quoted Genesis 19:24 to explain that I was wrong and Isaiah 1:10 to show that I could be righted in the event of conversion. They talked about the Father who was God and who was everywhere, I told them about mine who was also quite omnipresent.

"Who is it?"
"Some christo-nationalist Catholics, Papa!"
"Tell them to fuck off!"

You heard my father, I said to them sotto voce, he's no fan of clerics because of all the pedophiles in our good city of Lyon.

They replied with Luke 18:16 and, as I wasn't listening, they pushed on to the Epistle of Paul at Ephesus chapter 6 and, as that was driving me around the bend, they left to pursue their holy war on better plowed terrain.

I closed the door again, I felt liberated so I started going around in circles, and as I circled I was fretting even though I was free, I was anxious about being free even as I circled because of the distress of looking for a job and then of having a job if ever I found one, I went round and round and reread my "Arabic," I wondered why "Arabic" wasn't a job, thought to myself it was a question of profit not usefulness, you couldn't make a profit out of an "Arabic" and it had nothing to do with usefulness, whereas a *But Can You Not Understand That Life is Too Short* is useless in every way and sells rather well, fucking farce, I pondered the utility of poetry and reread one of my mother's reflections on Schiller:

> Usefulness limits the imagination
> The useful is opposed to the ideal
> Salaried work in service of the useful
> Freedom is on the side of the ideal without a use

An aesthetic education is an anti–mass-production education

We must not forget that Schiller was a citizen of his time.

I don't follow all of this, but I do suddenly realize that the usefulness of work is an old belief left over from Schiller's day. *Usefulness is the great icon of the era; she requires that all forces serve her and all talents pay her homage,* this is what he wrote in my mother's words, so that explains that, because in Schiller's day *you could still set useful things made to be sold against things not worth making because they do not sell,* that my mother had understood. After Schiller the poets lived with the dream of a dream so free it was absolutely ideal, and this ideal above the real, not the real on Earth but the ideal airborne in the limpid azure clarity, and you the poet altogether jobless, free of gravities, next to the sun you'd be the god shapeshifting between avatars or the child playing, that ideal child dreamed by the poet and their dreamt child-like pure poetry, fucking farce, obviously all that's dead and gone, it's been a good while that *useless things are produced and sell as well as anything else and children's dreams are the same as their parents'.* This my mother had understood.

Your mother is smart, shame she's crazy, my father said one day he'd been drinking.

I rolled a seriously stuffed one-rizla joint, listened to *Work, work, work, work, work, work, You see me* . . . so I could dance and make human noises as of the people I belong to, I drank one or two beers, or three, it's hazy, was it day or night, I don't know if I was on my bed, in my bed, well I thought of writing a poem about the orangs which are the utan people to which I belong, the nature of the orangs in a forest where Caterpillar tracks roll forward and the silent eyes of this great human people, it would finish like this, *animals cannot hate you*, well that was the idea. I could have written it if I'd felt like it but I chose to doze off in view of my state of intoxication. Drunk you write poetry, intoxicated you go to bed. I slept like a newt.

Next morning around midday, I made some coffee while the law on work which sets you free absorbed the expertise of my superego of a father. He was deep in his reading of the local newspapers from which he was drawing a series of lexicological studies, socio-economic commentaries, historical comparisons, political analyses, tactical tests and scholarly predictions, reciting accounts of the demo like State-sponsored poems:

Skirmishes
Broke out
In the region of three pm
Between some riot police and demonstrating
youths

Around Place Bellecour
At the edge of the crowd.

"What a bunch of animals!"
"Who, Papa?"
"Have you read Rilke?"
"Yes, but Rilke you know . . ."
"Reread him. You'll see."
"What will I see?"
"What he says about journalists and all those professions that aren't founded on anything real-life."
"Which professions?"
"The ones people call artistic which, while mimicking art, actually undercut and insult it. Well, it's not all about that, I'm going to go away for a while to bronze my backside in the Cayman Islands."

He was already packing his suitcase, there were heaps of Hawaiian shirts, his Plato collection and his baby oil for men, when suddenly he looked up.

"You're not going for an artistic profession, are you?"
"A profession? You mean something so I can get a job? No, Papa."
"Good. Because you'd do better to . . ."
"Have a great time, Papa."

10

For the next few days I had things to do, I think I was living and I lived like that without thinking about work, I was living to be alive, not to earn my living because there are so many of us, we the orang people, living without earning. I wrote something on the monkey in men but I didn't finish it, you need time to see in back of the real.

It was almost April, I had no job, I was able to work, I was writing reams and smoking in moderation, I was in a good mood. I shelved Klemperer and Kraus next to Kafka—Kafka now, I recalled, it was the *Letter to his Father* that I'd read weeping my heart out in the pathos of my mother's death, so that explains that.

I reread the beginning:

Dearest Father,
You asked me recently why I maintain that I am afraid of you.

I fell about laughing under the influence of my drug, Kafka had a good sense of humor, we always forget that, right from the start Kafka's sense of humour is crazy joyful.

As usual, I was unable to think of any answer to your question, partly for the very reason that I am afraid of you, and partly because an explanation of the grounds for this fear would mean going into far more details than I could even approximately keep in mind while talking.

He's brilliant, our Kafka, there's no one like him in the whole population of this great ape people of ours.

And if I now try to give you an answer in writing, it will still be very incomplete, because, even in writing, this fear and its consequences hamper me in relation to you and because the magnitude of the subject goes far beyond the scope of my memory and power of reasoning.

The opening lines of the *Letter to his Father* have of course been analyzed by dozens of Kafkaists, of course there are hundreds of expert literary analyses of the *Letter to his Father*, this *Letter to his Father* was on the reading lists in all the universities of Bologna and Navarra, and all I have to say personally is that I could die laughing, *I maintain I am afraid*, oh it's priceless!

"I don't think so."

"*This fear would mean going into far too much detail—*that's really funny, Papa."

"So-so."

"And *the magnitude of the subject,* that bit too, properly laugh-out-loud, don't you think?"

"I don't see anything funny about it."

I didn't go on, I'd already got plenty out of those three lines, enough for the rest of my life.

Besides, I had to go out to oppose the use of work in solidarity with the utan people to which I belong, the wind was in the south, the helicopters were hovering, the shops were closed for the love of all things, I was walking in the good city of Lyon, someone among everyone, one person among us, loiterers against the law, the riot police buses and the State ordinaries were turning into our street.

There's a fair bit of poetry at the moment, I said to my father.

He didn't reply.

NOÉMI LEFEBVRE was born in 1964 in Caen, and now lives in Lyon, France. She studied music for over 10 years as a child and later obtained her PhD on the subject of music education and national identity in Germany and France. She became a political scientist at CERAT de Grenoble II Institute. She is the author of four novels, including *Blue Self-Portrait* and *Poetics of Work*, all of which have garnered intense critical success.

SOPHIE LEWIS is a literary editor and translator from French and Portuguese into English. She has translated Stendhal, Jules Verne, Marcel Aymé, Violette Leduc, Emmanuelle Pagano, and João Gilberto Noll, among others.

Transit Books is a nonprofit publisher of international and American literature, based in Oakland, California. Founded in 2015, Transit Books is committed to the discovery and promotion of enduring works that carry readers across borders and communities. Visit us online to learn more about our forthcoming titles, events, and opportunities to support our mission.

TRANSITBOOKS.ORG